Published by Ladybird Books Ltd Loughborough Leicestershire UK
Ladybird Books Inc Lewiston Maine 04240 USA

Printed in England

Old King Cole

and other nursery rhymes

Illustrated by KEN McKIE

Ladybird Books

Old King Cole
Was a merry old soul,
And a merry old soul was he;
He called for his pipe,
And he called for his bowl,
And he called for his fiddlers three.

Hickory, dickory, dock,
The mouse ran up the clock.
The clock struck one,
The mouse was gone,
Hickory, dickory, dock.

Georgie Porgie,
pudding and pie,

Kissed the girls
and made them cry;

When the boys came
out to play,

Georgie Porgie ran away.

Little Miss Muffet
Sat on a tuffet,
Eating her curds and whey;
There came a big spider,
Who sat down beside her
And frightened Miss Muffet away.

Diddle, diddle, dumpling,
my son John,
Went to bed
with his trousers on;

One shoe off
and the other shoe on,

Diddle, diddle, dumpling,
my son John.

*H*ush-a-bye, baby,
on the tree top,

When the wind blows,
the cradle will rock;

When the bough breaks,
the cradle will fall,

Down will come baby,
cradle and all.

Pease porridge hot,
Pease porridge cold,
Pease porridge in the pot,
Nine days old.

Some like it hot,
Some like it cold,
Some like it in the pot,
Nine days old.

*L*ittle Tommy Tucker,
Sings for his supper:
What shall we give him?
White bread and butter.
How will he cut it
Without a knife?
How will he marry
Without a wife?

*Ride a cock-horse
        to Banbury Cross,*

*To see a fine lady
        upon a white horse;*

*Rings on her fingers
        and bells on her toes,*

*She shall have music
        wherever she goes.*

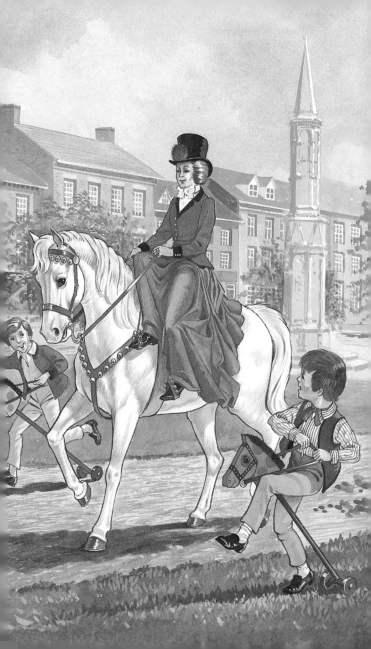

Tom, Tom, the piper's son,
Stole a pig and away did run;
The pig was eat
And Tom was beat,
And Tom went howling down
the street.

Hot cross buns!
Hot cross buns!
One a penny, two a penny,
Hot cross buns!
If you have no daughters,
Give them to your sons,
One a penny, two a penny
Hot cross buns!

Mary, Mary, quite contrary,
How does your garden grow?
With silver bells and cockle shells
And pretty maids all in a row.

Yankee Doodle came to town,
Riding on a pony;
He stuck a feather in his cap
And called it macaroni.

Jack Sprat could eat no fat,
His wife could eat no lean,
And so between them both, you see,
They licked the platter clean.

Doctor Foster went to Gloucester
In a shower of rain;
He stepped in a puddle,
Right up to his middle,
And never went there again.

*Old Mother Hubbard
Went to the cupboard,
To get her poor dog a bone;
But when she got there
The cupboard was bare
And so the poor dog had none.*

*H*iggledy Piggledy, my black hen,
She lays eggs for gentlemen;
Sometimes nine and sometimes ten
Higgledy Piggledy, my black hen.

The Queen of Hearts
She made some tarts,
All on a summer's day;
The Knave of Hearts
He stole the tarts,
And took them right away.

The King of Hearts,
Called for the tarts,
And beat the Knave full sore;
The Knave of Hearts
Brought back the tarts,
And vowed he'd steal no more.

Rub-a-dub-dub,

Three men in a tub,

And how do you think
they got there?

The butcher, the baker,

The candlestick-maker,

They all jumped out of a
rotten potato,

'Twas enough to make a man stare.

Curly-locks, Curly-locks,
Wilt thou be mine?
Thou shalt not wash dishes
Nor yet feed the swine,
But sit on a cushion
And sew a fine seam,
And feed upon strawberries,
Sugar and cream.